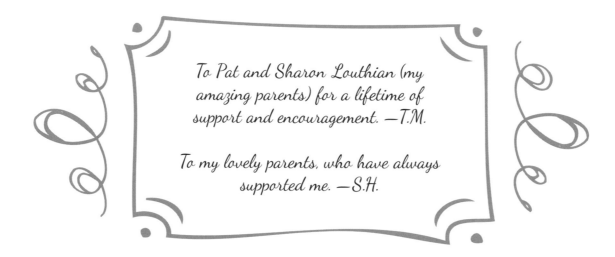

To Pat and Sharon Louthian (my amazing parents) for a lifetime of support and encouragement. —T.M.

To my lovely parents, who have always supported me. —S.H.

Published by Familius™ LLC, www.familius.com

Familius books are available at special discounts for bulk purchases, whether for sales promotions or for family or corporate use. For more information, contact Premium Sales at 559-876-2170 or email orders@familius.com.

Library of Congress Cataloging-in-Publication Data
2017942645   ISBN 9781945547119

Printed in China

Book and jacket design by David Miles
Edited by Lindsay Sandberg

10 9 8 7 6 5 4 3 2 1

First Edition

12 Little Elves visit CALiForNiA

BY TRISH MADSON

ILLUSTRATIONS BY
SADIE HAN

FAMILIUS

’T was Christmas in California
and 12 elves were sent
to see who was sleeping . . .

away the elves went!

In each home was nestled each girl and each boy,

PACIFIC
OCEAN

while Golden State visions brought everyone joy.

FISHERMANS WHARF · OF SAN FRANCISCO ·

On Fisherman's Wharf
crabs sang "Silent Night,"
and lobsters chimed in:
"All is calm, all is bright."

Grizzlies took turns riding wintery sleds
while campers saw sugarplums dance in their heads.

Union Square sparkled with
red and green lights,

and traffic turned into a huge snowball fight.

Santa landed his sleigh
at the Hollywood Bowl
just in time to replenish
his stockpile of coal.

Los Angeles bustled with
last-minute shoppers,
and the Walk of Fame stars
shone like Christmas tree toppers.

Yosemite sparkled
like a white wonderland.

But reindeer danced merrily
in the warm coastal sand.

★ SANTA CRUZ

PACIFIC
OCEAN

From Pismo to Santa Cruz,
the surfers spread cheer,
putting tinsel and lights
on the boardwalk and pier.

★ PISMO

The redwoods were dazzling
with red lights and bows—
a perfect new home for
Rudolph and his nose.

Goodnight, California.
You're all fast asleep,
but there's just one more house
that the elves want to see . . .

Hurry to bed and shut your eyes tight.
Merry Christmas, dear California.
12 elves say goodnight!